Where is Patch?

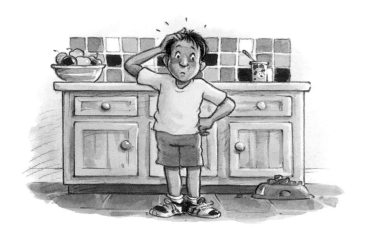

Anne Bauers

Illustrated by Steve Smallman

RIGBY

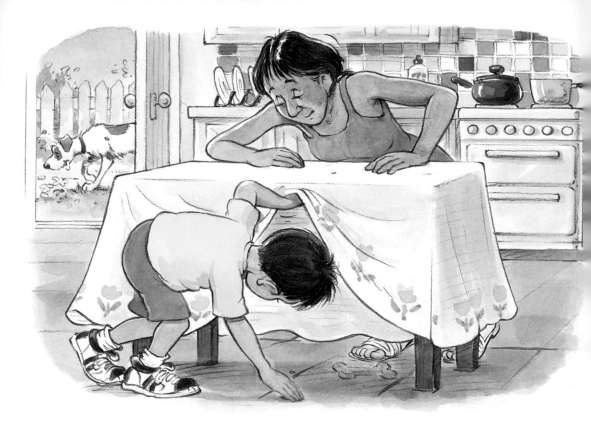

Is he in the kitchen?

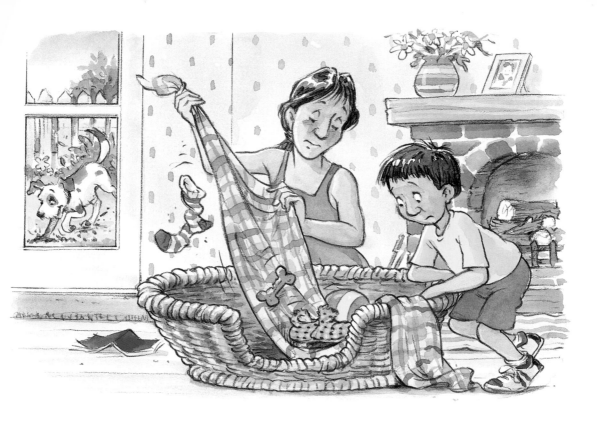

Is he in the basket?

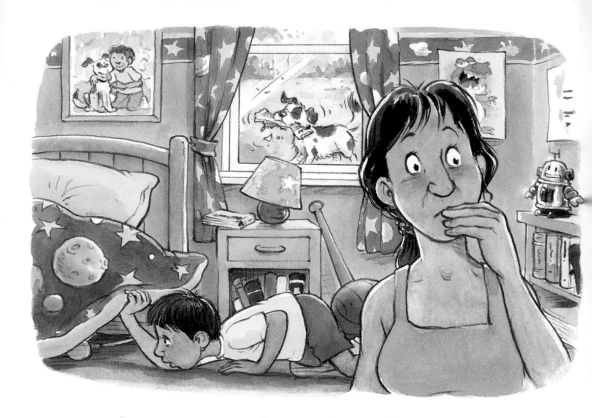

Is he in the bedroom?

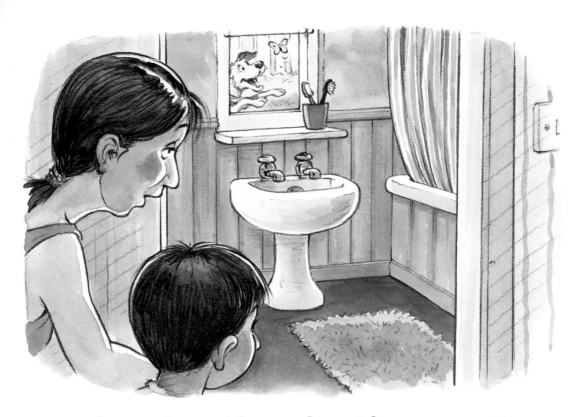

Is he in the bathroom?

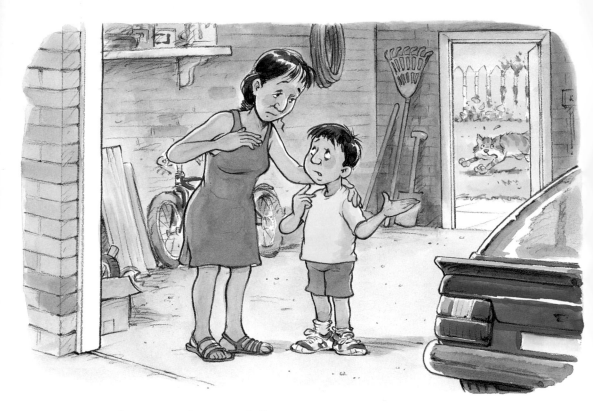

Is he in the garage?

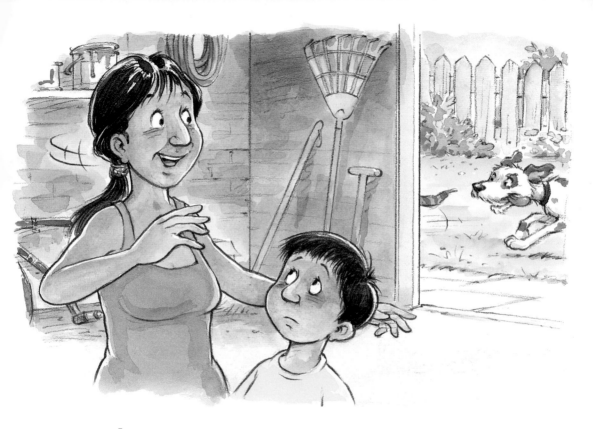

Look . . .

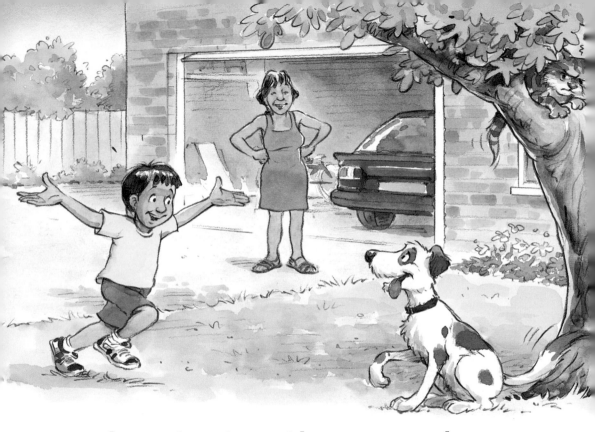

he is in the garden!